Dear Gran and Grandpa
We are having a good time.
We like the beach and go
swimming every day. We
have been to the fun fair,
too. Yesterday we bought
sombreros because the
sun is very hot. The ice
cream is great.

Love,

Kim and Jim

Gran and Grandpa
Drummond Street

Consultant Gussie Hearsey on behalf of the Pre-school Playgroups Association
©1987 Maureen Roffey
Four Winds Press
Macmillan Publishing Company
866 Third Avenue, New York, NY 10022
First published 1987 in Great Britain by Walker Books Ltd, London,
under the title *I Spy on Holiday*
First American Edition 1988
Printed in Hong Kong by Dai Nippon (H.K.) Ltd.

10 9 8 7 6 5 4 3 2 1

Library of Congress Cataloging-in-Publication Data
Roffey, Maureen.
I spy on vacation.
Summary: Readers may finish sentences by saying
what they "spy" in pictures of a beach vacation.
[1. Seashore—Fiction] I. Title.
PZ7.R6255Iaf 1988   [E]   87-12115
ISBN 0-02-777160-1

I SPY
On Vacation

Maureen Roffey

FOUR WINDS PRESS · NEW YORK

I spy the sea.

HOTEL

I spy a pair of sunglasses on the…

I spy a man reading a...

I spy a round, striped...

I spy twelve gray and white…

I spy a white sun hat with a yellow...

I spy the waiter bringing two...

I spy a bumper car going…

I spy our friends waving from the...

HOTEL

I spy the conveyor belt carrying four...

I spy two children playing…

27

I spy Grandma and Grandpa waiting for us.

TANGIER
CL37 PARIS
PA51 MIAMI
BA72 ATHENS
ES36 BARCELONA
AL35 FLORENCE

Arrivals

29